The Face Thief

She Borrows Faces to Save Lives

P. A. Farrell

ISBN: 979-8-9937396-3-2

Cover photo: gavrilukph@unsplash

The Pocket Companion Series contains:

When Your Mind Won't Stop

After the Loss: Finding Your Way Through Grief

You Are Enough: Rebuilding Your Self-Worth

At the Crossroads: Making Decisions When Nothing Feels Clear

When People Hurt: Navigating Difficult Relationships

When You Feel Stuck: Finding Movement in Hard Times

Books by Patricia A. Farrell, Ph.D.

When You Can't Pour From an Empty Glass: CBT Skills for Exhausted Caregivers

The Little Book on Learning Big Critical Thinking Skills

The Smart Kid's Survival Guide: Making Good Choices in a Confusing World

P. A. FARRELL

How to Be Your Own Therapist

It's Not All in Your Head: Anxiety, Depression, Mood Swings and Multiple Sclerosis

Unfiltered: Beneath the noise of our thoughts lies the true narrative of our minds

Unfiltered Again: A behind-the-scenes look at healthcare, medicine and mental health

A Social Security Disability Psychological Claims Handbook: A simple guide to understanding your SSD claim for psychological impairments and unraveling the maze of decision-making

A Social Security Disability Psychological Claims Guidebook for Children's Benefits

The Disability Accessible US Parks in All 50 States: A Comprehensive Guide

Birding in the US NOW!: A birding guide for individuals with disabilities

Contents

Chapter 1: The last face she wore

Morgan Hayes pressed her palm against the bathroom mirror and watched her reflection blur. The glass went cold under her hand. Frost spread from her fingertips in tiny white veins, branching across the surface like frozen lightning. She'd done this a hundred times, maybe more, but the cold still surprised her. Still made her breath catch.

The apartment was quiet except for the hum of traffic outside and the muffled sounds of the bakery below. Morgan lived above Jenna's family bakery in downtown Cedar Falls. The smell of fresh bread rose through the floorboards every morning at five. She'd gotten used to it. Learned to love it, even. It was the smell of something real. Something that didn't change. Something that held a promise of delight and pleasurable eating.

Morgan closed her hazel eyes and thought about the woman sitting in her living room. Claire Martinez. Twenty-eight years old. Office manager at a dental practice. Brown eyes. Dark hair that fell just past her shoulders. A small mole on her left cheek, barely visible. The shape of her nose, slightly upturned at the tip. The curve of her jaw, delicate but strong. The way her mouth turned down at the corners when she was nervous, which was most of the time lately.

She'd spent the last hour studying Claire's face, memorizing every detail. The way her eyebrows arched, the faint scar above her right eye from a childhood accident, and the exact shade of brown in her eyes, warm like honey in sunlight. You had to get it all right; every detail mattered.

The cold spread through Morgan's body. It always started in her chest, right behind her ribs. A deep freeze that moved outward through her veins like ice water. It reached her shoulders, her arms, and her hands. Then up her neck to her face. That was when the real change happened. It was happening now.

Her bones ached as they shifted. Not breaking, exactly. More like bending. Reshaping themselves to match the face she was borrowing. Her skin felt like it was being pulled tight, then loosened, then pulled again. Her cheekbones shifted higher. Her jaw narrowed. Her nose changed shape. Soon she'd be ready.

The sensation only lasted about fifteen seconds, but it felt longer. It felt like drowning in cold water while your body turned into someone else's. Morgan had never gotten used to it. She didn't think she ever would. It was something she was expecting.

When Morgan opened her eyes, Claire Martinez stared back at her from the mirror.

Same brown eyes. Same dark hair, falling past her shoulders in soft waves. Same nervous mouth, turned down slightly at the corners. Same mole on the left cheek. Even Morgan's height had changed. She was shorter now, maybe five-four instead of five-seven. Her clothes hung differently on the smaller frame, looser at the shoulders, tighter at the hips. Ready or not, here she was coming.

Morgan touched her face with Claire's hands. Smaller hands, narrower fingers. She ran them over her cheeks, her nose, her jaw. Everything felt wrong and right at the same time. Like wearing someone else's skin, which was exactly what she was doing.

She took a breath and walked back into the living room. Her footsteps sounded different—lighter. That was always strange, too—how your whole body changes, not just your face. The way you move. The way you carry yourself. You become them, completely. Yes, completely them in every way.

Claire sat on the couch, hands twisted in her lap. She'd been crying earlier. Her eyes were still red, puffy. When she looked up and saw herself standing in the doorway, she gasped. Actually gasped, like someone had punched the air out of her lungs.

"It's weird, isn't it?" Morgan said in Claire's voice. That was the part that always freaked people out the most. Not just the face, but the voice too. Everything changed. The pitch, the tone, the way words shaped themselves in your mouth. Morgan sounded exactly like Claire now. Even she could hear it.

Claire stood up slowly, still staring. She took a step forward, then stopped. "I can't believe it. You look exactly like me."

"That's the point."

"How do you do it? How is this even possible?"

Morgan shrugged Claire's shoulders. "I don't know. I was born like this. Figured it out when I was a kid. Scared my parents half to death when I turned into my sister one day." She knew more than she was willing to reveal at this moment, so the cover story would have to be enough for now.

"Does it hurt?"

"A little. But I'm used to it." That was a lie. It always hurt. But Claire didn't need to know that. She was suffering enough and she didn't need to hear that Morgan was in any type of distress.

Claire walked closer, studying Morgan's face. Her own face. "How long will it hold?"

"Six hours, maybe eight if I concentrate. Plenty of time to get you out of Cedar Falls."

"And he'll think you're me. Travis will follow you." Morgan had been through this many times and she knew this guy would follow her.

"That's the plan. While he's watching me, you'll be long gone."

Claire's ex-boyfriend, Travis, had been watching her apartment for three days—sitting in his truck across the street, following her to work, calling her phone twenty times a day, and leaving messages that started sweet but ended with threats. The restraining order didn't stop him, and the police couldn't do anything until he actually hurt her. By then, it would be too late. Numerous stories in newspapers detailed women stalked by ex-boyfriends or husbands seeking police protection, and in most cases, they were killed. She didn't want this to be happen to her and there had to be a way out that Morgan was now offering.

So Claire called a friend who knew someone who knew someone who had Morgan's number. That was how it always worked. Word of mouth. Whispered recommendations. People who were desperate enough to believe in something impossible.

Morgan didn't advertise. She didn't have a website or business cards. No social media presence. Nothing that could be traced back to her. People found her when they needed her, and only when they were truly desperate. When they needed to disappear, just for a little while. When they needed someone else to be them, this wasn't a game, it was deadly serious life.

"You sure about this?" Claire asked. Her voice was shaking. "I mean, what if he gets violent? What if he realizes you're not me and—"

Morgan held up a hand. "I've done this before. You're not the first person who needed to vanish for a day. I know what I'm doing."

"But Travis, he's not like other guys. He has a temper. When we were together, he—" Claire stopped, swallowing hard. "He hurt me. More than once."

"I know," Morgan mumbled. Claire had told her everything during their first meeting. The bruises Travis left. The broken ribs. The night she finally left, running out the door with nothing but her purse and her car keys. "That's why we're doing this. He needs to think you're still here. Needs to waste his time following me around Cedar Falls. By the time he figures it out, you'll be in another state."

Claire took a shaky breath. "What if he corners you? What if he tries to—"

"He won't know it's not you until my face shifts back. And by then, I'll be long gone. I'm good at disappearing."

Claire nodded, but she didn't look convinced. Morgan didn't blame her. This whole thing sounded crazy. It was crazy. But it worked. Morgan had helped dozens of people over the years. Abused partners. Stalking victims. People who needed a clean break but couldn't get one on their own. She'd been there for all of them.

"Thank you," Claire said. "I don't know how to pay you for this. I mean, two hundred dollars doesn't seem like enough. Not for the risk you're taking." It was her usual fee and she never asked for more than that.

"You already paid me. It's enough." Morgan had asked for two hundred dollars. Just enough to cover her time and the risk. Not enough to make it feel like a business. This wasn't about money. It never had been. It was about helping people who had no other options. People the system had failed. If the system couldn't work in their favor for people in jeopardy, then she was going to do it.

Claire picked up her bag from the couch. It was a worn canvas duffel, stuffed full of clothes and whatever else she'd managed to grab from her apartment. Everything she owned now, packed into one bag. "There's a bus at four. Leaves from the station on Main Street. Goes to Des Moines." Freedom was waiting for her at that plus depot. "Good. Stay on it until you're out of Iowa. Find a small town. Somewhere Travis won't think to look."

"My cousin lives in Nebraska. She said I could stay with her for a while." The hesitation in her voice told Morgan that Clare wasn't sure, and she needed to let Claire know this was a good plan.

"Perfect. But don't tell anyone else where you're going. Not your friends. Not your family. No one." Some secrets really need to be kept and Morgan knew that. As she spoke, Morgan turned her head slightly to further emphasize that this secret must remain confidential. A slight nod solidified it.

"I won't." Claire hesitated at the door, her hand on the knob. "What about you? I mean, after today. What if Travis comes looking for you? What if he figures out who you really are?" So many questions she'd heard before but Morgan knew everyone in this situation who had a heart was concerned for her safety as well as their own.

"He won't. By the time my face shifts back, I'll be gone. He'll just think he saw things. That stress made him see something that wasn't there. People convince themselves of all kinds of things when reality doesn't make sense."

Claire nodded one last time and opened the door. She looked back at Morgan, at her own face staring back at her. "Thank you. Really. You're saving my life."

Then she was gone. Morgan listened to her footsteps fade away as she went down the stairs, heard the outside door open and close. The apartment was quiet again. Just Morgan and the distant sounds of the bakery below. The steady rhythm of baking. Mixing, kneading, rising, baking. Simple. Predictable.

Morgan looked down at her hands. Claire's hands. Small, with short nails painted pale pink. There was a thin scar on the left thumb from a kitchen accident. Morgan studied it, running her right thumb over the scar tissue. Every detail was perfect. Every detail had to be perfect.

She had six hours to be Claire Martinez. Six hours to lead a dangerous man on a wild chase through Cedar Falls. Six hours to keep him busy while the real Claire got away. Caution was the watchword, and planning was essential.

Morgan checked her reflection in the hallway mirror once more. Claire's face stared back—nervous and scared. The corners of her mouth turned down. Her eyes were wide with fear. It was perfect. Just how Claire would look if she was about to step outside and face her abuser.

Morgan grabbed Claire's jacket from the hook by the door. Navy blue, worn at the elbows. She put it on, feeling how it fit differently on this smaller body. She picked up Claire's purse. Black leather, heavy with a wallet, keys, phone. All the things that made someone real. All the things that made someone traceable.

Time to go to work.

Chapter 2: The woman in the corner booth

Morgan left her apartment twenty minutes later. She took her time, moving like Claire would move—slowly, carefully, glancing over her shoulder every few steps. A woman who knew someone was watching. A woman who was scared. Yes, she knew the drill.

She wore Claire's jacket and carried Claire's purse. The weight of it felt strange on her shoulder, but she adjusted. She even walked like Claire—shoulders slightly hunched forward, eyes down, small steps. The posture of someone who had learned to make herself smaller, to take up less space in the world.

People saw what they expected to see. If you looked like someone, sounded like someone, or moved like someone, you were considered that person. That was the key. It wasn't just about the face; it was about everything—the whole package.

The street outside was busy. Mid-afternoon in Cedar Falls. People walking dogs. Mothers pushing strollers. Students from the community college heading to class. Normal life. The kind of life Morgan usually watched from the sidelines. Now, however, she was enmeshed in the street life here.

Travis was waiting across the street, exactly where Claire said he'd be. Morgan spotted him immediately. Tall guy, maybe six-two. Broad shoulders, thick arms. Wearing a baseball cap pulled low over his face and sunglasses even though it wasn't sunny out in the open. He was leaning against a pickup truck, pretending to look at his phone. But Morgan could feel his attention. Could feel him watching. He was watching her.

Morgan kept her head down and walked toward Main Street. Her heart was pounding, but she kept her pace steady. Claire's pace. Not too fast. Not too slow. Just a woman running errands. Nothing unusual. Nothing to see here.

She felt Travis's eyes on her back. Heavy. Intense. The kind of stare that made your skin crawl. Morgan forced herself not to look back. Claire wouldn't look back. Claire would be too scared to acknowledge him. Too scared to make eye contact. She kept reminding herself to act like Claire. Nothing must be out of the ordinary now.

Good. Let him follow. Let him think he'd found her. Let him waste his time. Time was the important commodity, and she had to be sure that he wasted a lot of it following her.

Morgan spent the next hour leading him on a pointless tour of Cedar Falls. First stop was the grocery store on Fifth Street. She went inside and bought a gallon of milk she didn't need. She took her time, wandering the aisles, picking up items and putting them back. Playing the part. Being Claire Martinez, living her normal life, pretending she didn't know someone was watching.

Through the store windows, she could see Travis's truck parked across the street. He hadn't bothered to hide it. Didn't need to. He wanted Claire to know he was there. Wanted her to be scared. That was how guys like him operated. Fear was the weapon, and he knew it. It's probably the way he had acted with most women in his life.

Next, Morgan stopped at the post office. She mailed an empty envelope to a random address. Stood in line for fifteen minutes just to waste time. Then she walked past Claire's workplace, the dental office on Maple Street. She didn't go in; she just slowed down as she walked by. Let Travis see her looking at the building. Let him think she was considering going to work.

He followed at a distance, never getting too close. Always half a block behind. Sometimes on the opposite side of the street. Sometimes in his truck, crawling along at five miles per hour. He probably thought he was being subtle. Thought Claire wouldn't notice.

But Morgan had spent years learning to notice when someone was watching her. You had to, in her line of work. You had to develop eyes in the back of your head. Had to feel the weight of someone's attention before they got too close. It was a survival skill. One she'd learned the hard way. Yes, there had been instances where she had been deficient in her observations of someone and she did pay a price for it.

By the time she circled back toward the apartment, Claire would be at the bus station. Morgan checked the time on Claire's phone. Three forty-five. The bus left at four. Fifteen minutes. Just fifteen more minutes and Claire would be safe.

Morgan ducked into a coffee shop called The Daily Grind. Small place, local, the kind with mismatched furniture and art from local painters on the walls. She ordered a latte and sat by the window. Travis's truck pulled up outside a minute later. He parked right across the street, not even trying to hide anymore. Now he was sitting there feeling very confident that he had cornered her.

Morgan pretended to read a book she'd grabbed from a shelf near the door. Some romance novel with a couple embracing on the cover. She didn't actually read any of it. Just turned pages every few minutes. Her eyes were on the reflection in the window. Watching Travis watch her.

The hands on the clock on the wall moved slowly forward. Four o'clock. Four-fifteen. Four-thirty. The bus would be gone by now. Claire would be on it, heading south, heading away from Cedar Falls and Travis and everything that had hurt her. Hopefully everything had gone right for Claire.

Morgan felt the first pull at four forty-five. The face was starting to slip. It always happened like this. No warning, just a subtle shift in the way her skin felt. Like wearing a mask that didn't quite fit anymore. Like something was tugging at the edges, trying to peel it away.

She touched her face with Claire's hand. The features felt less solid now. More fluid. She had maybe thirty minutes before the change became obvious. Before Claire's face melted away and Morgan's emerged underneath.

Time to go and in a hurry.

Morgan left her coffee half-finished and walked out the back door of the shop. There was an alley behind the building, narrow and shadowed. Dumpsters lined one side. The back doors of other businesses lined the other. Morgan moved quickly now, Claire's small legs carrying her faster than before. She heard Travis's footsteps behind her a moment later. Heavier. Faster. He wasn't being subtle anymore.

"Claire!" His voice echoed off the brick walls. Angry. Desperate. "Claire, wait!"

Morgan kept walking. The alley opened onto a side street. She could see her car parked half a block away. Her real car, not Claire's.

She'd parked it there this morning, knowing she'd need a quick escape route.

"I just want to talk!" Travis was closer now. Morgan could hear his breathing, heavy and ragged. "Claire, stop! You can't just walk away from me!"

Morgan reached her car and fumbled with Claire's small hands for the keys. Her fingers felt clumsy, unfamiliar. The keys slipped. She caught them. Tried again.

Travis grabbed her arm just as she got the door open. His grip was tight. Painful. His fingers dug into her skin hard enough to bruise.

"Let go," Morgan said in Claire's voice. Firm but scared. The way Claire would sound.

"Not until you listen to me." His face was inches from hers. Morgan could smell stale coffee and cigarettes on his breath. Could see the veins standing out in his neck, the red flush of anger creeping up from his collar. "You can't just walk away from this. From us. We're not done, Claire. We'll never be done." That was more than a warning. That was a threat.

Morgan felt Claire's face slipping faster now. The cold was spreading through her body again, but this time it was different. This time it was pulling the face away, not holding it in place. The adrenaline had broken her concentration. Had disrupted whatever strange biology made this ability work.

Travis's eyes widened as Morgan's face began to change. First the eyes. Brown shifted to hazel, the color bleeding out like watercolor paint. Then the hair. Dark brown faded to auburn, lightening strand by strand. The shape of her jaw softened. Her nose narrowed. Her cheekbones shifted lower. In the space of maybe ten seconds, Claire Martinez disappeared completely.

Travis stumbled backward, his hand dropping from her arm. His mouth fell open. His face went pale, then red, then pale again. He looked like he might throw up. Or pass out. Or both.

"What the hell?" His voice was barely a whisper. "What the hell was that?"

Morgan got in her car and locked the door. She started the engine. Looked at Travis through the window. He was just standing there, frozen, staring at her with wide, terrified eyes.

"Wrong person," Morgan said. Her own voice now. Higher than Claire's. Different tone. Different everything. "You followed the wrong person."

She drove away before he could recover. In the rearview mirror, she watched him stand there in the middle of the street, confused and scared. His whole world had just tilted sideways. Reality had stopped making sense.

Good. Maybe now he'd leave Claire alone. Maybe now he'd think twice before showing up at her apartment. Maybe he'd be too scared of what he'd seen to keep stalking her. Maybe he'd convince himself it was stress. That grief and anger had made him hallucinate. That faces didn't just change like that.

People believed what they needed to believe. And Travis needed to believe he was losing his mind more than he needed to believe in someone like Morgan.

Morgan drove home through the quiet streets of Cedar Falls. The afternoon was fading into evening. The sky was turning in those wonderful evening hues at the edges. She felt tired. Bone-deep tired. The kind of exhaustion that came from wearing someone else's skin for too long. She needed to rest.

Back at her apartment, she went straight to the bathroom. She pressed her hands against the mirror and watched her own reflection solidify. Auburn hair, shoulder-length and wavy. Hazel eyes with flecks of green and gold. The small scar on her chin from a bike accident when she was ten. She touched it with her own fingers, feeling the familiar ridge of scar tissue.

She was Morgan Hayes again. Completely herself. No borrowed features. No stolen identity.

And somewhere, hopefully far away by now, Claire Martinez was safe.

That was what mattered. That was why Morgan did this.

Chapter 3: The shift back

The lawyer showed up three days later, on a Wednesday morning. Morgan was eating breakfast at the small table by the window, watching the street below come alive with morning traffic. People heading to work. Kids walking to school. The normal rhythm of life in Cedar Falls.

Someone knocked on her door. Sharp, professional knocks. Not the tentative tap of someone asking for help. Morgan set down her coffee and looked through the peephole. A woman stood in the hallway. Mid-forties, wearing a gray suit that probably cost more than Morgan's rent. She carried a leather briefcase and had the kind of posture that came from years of confidence. Authority.

Morgan opened the door but kept the chain lock engaged. "Can I help you?" Peering out at the woman, she couldn't figure out what business she would have here.

"Morgan Hayes?" the woman asked. She had a calm, measured voice. The kind of voice that was used to being listened to.

"Depends who's asking."

The woman reached into her jacket and pulled out a badge. Morgan's stomach sank. "My name is Karen Lindstrom. I'm an attorney with the U.S. Attorney's Office, Eastern District of Iowa. Can I come in? I promise this isn't what you think."

Morgan hesitated. Federal lawyers didn't show up at your door unless something was very wrong. Unless you were in trouble. Unless they wanted something. But Karen's face didn't have that look. She wasn't here to arrest anyone. Morgan could read people. It was part of the job. Part of surviving.

"What's this about?" Morgan asked, still not opening the door all the way. Some clarification was called for, and she was going to ask for it.

"I'd rather discuss it inside. Please. It's about a job. One that could help save someone's life." Save someone's life? That was a curious request.

Morgan studied Karen's face for another moment, then unhooked the chain and let her in. Karen stepped inside and looked around the apartment. Taking it all in. The small kitchen with mismatched chairs. The living room with its secondhand couch. The walls bare except for a few photos. It was clean but sparse. The home of someone who traveled light. Someone who might need to leave in a hurry. For a brief, moment she wondered why it was so sparse but then she dismissed it.

Karen sat on the couch and set her briefcase on the coffee table. She opened it and pulled out a folder. Manila, thick with papers. "I'll get right to the point, Ms. Hayes. We have a witness in protective custody. A woman named Beth Warner. She's testifying against a criminal organization. Money laundering, racketeering, murder. Big case. Dangerous people. We need to keep her safe until the trial. That's where you come in."

Morgan stayed standing, arms crossed. "How do you know about me?" That was the important question. The one that mattered. Morgan was careful. She didn't leave traces. Didn't advertise. How had the federal government found her? But then the government had its ways, and it was obvious one of them had opened up and given her name to them.

Karen smiled slightly. "We've been watching you for a while. Not officially. No surveillance, no warrants. But people talk. Especially people we've helped in other cases. A woman named Sarah Meadows. Do you remember her?"

Morgan did remember. Sarah had been running from an abusive husband who was a cop. She'd needed to disappear completely. Morgan had worn her face for six hours while Sarah got on a plane to California. That had been almost a year ago. "Yeah, I remember."

"She's alive because of you. Her husband never found her. She started over. Got a new job. New life. And she mentioned to one of our victim advocates that she'd had help. Unusual help. We looked into it. Very quietly. Very carefully. We know what you can do, Ms. Hayes."

Morgan's jaw tightened. "And you want me to do the same thing for your witness. Be her. Draw the bad guys away while she stays hidden."

"Exactly. We need someone in her apartment for three days. Just long enough to make it look like she's still there. Anyone watching will think they've found her. Meanwhile, the real Beth Warner will be in a secure location. Safe."

"What happens when they come after me?" Morgan asked. Because they would come. If these people were as dangerous as Karen said, they wouldn't just watch. They'd act.

"We'll have agents nearby. Two in a van across the street. One in the building next door. You'll have a panic button. Press it and help arrives in thirty seconds. You'll be protected. I promise."

Morgan shook her head. "I don't do jobs like this. I help people escape bad relationships. Stalkers. Abusive partners. Dangerous exes. Not federal cases. Not organized crime. That's way outside my wheelhouse."

Karen leaned forward. "Beth Warner is a single mother. Two kids. Seven and nine years old. She was working as an administrative assistant for a company called Midwest Holdings. One night, she stayed late to finish some paperwork. She saw her boss murder someone in his office. Shot him twice in the chest. Beth ran. Called 911. Did everything right. And now her family's in danger because she had the courage to come forward and testify."

Morgan looked out the window. The street below was busy. People living their lives. Going to work. Running errands. Normal people in a normal town. Beth Warner had been normal too. Until she saw something she shouldn't have seen.

"We're offering you fifty thousand dollars," Karen said quietly. "To help us keep her safe."

Fifty thousand. Morgan turned back to look at Karen. That was more money than she'd ever made in a year. More money than she'd ever seen in one place. That was rent for two years. Maybe three if she was careful. That was security. That was freedom from worrying about money for a long time.

But something felt wrong about this. The federal government didn't need someone like Morgan. They had entire departments dedicated to witness protection. Safe houses in every state. Trained agents. Resources Morgan couldn't even imagine. Why would they need a twenty-nine-year-old woman with a strange ability and no formal training?

"There's something you're not telling me," Morgan said. She could see it in Karen's face. The slight tightness around her eyes. The way she wasn't quite meeting Morgan's gaze.

Karen was quiet for a moment. Then she sighed. "The people looking for Beth Warner are dangerous. Professional. They've already found two of our safe houses. We think there might be a leak in the system. Someone feeding them information. We don't know who. We don't know how deep it goes. So we're trying something different. Something they won't expect. Something completely off the books."

"You're using me as bait," Morgan said flatly.

Karen didn't deny it. "We're using you as a decoy. And yes, it's dangerous. I won't lie to you about that. But Beth Warner's life depends on it. Her children's lives depend on it. If they find her before the trial, she's dead. Her kids are orphans. And a very dangerous man walks free."

Morgan looked at the folder on the coffee table. Inside would be a photo of Beth Warner. A woman she'd never met. A woman whose face she'd have to wear for three days while trained killers tried to find her. While professional criminals hunted her. This was different from helping Claire escape her ex-boyfriend. This was different from any job she'd ever done. This was federal. This was real danger.

But fifty thousand dollars. And two kids who needed their mother to survive. Two kids who'd done nothing wrong except have a mom who saw something terrible and decided to do the right thing.

Morgan took a deep breath. Let it out slowly. "Three days. That's it. And your agents better be as close as you say they are."

Karen's face relaxed. She actually smiled. "They will be. I promise. Thank you, Ms. Hayes. You're doing a good thing here."

She opened the folder and pulled out a photo. Eight by ten, color, high quality. Beth Warner. Blonde hair cut in a short bob. Blue eyes. A tired smile that didn't quite reach those eyes. Maybe thirty-five. Pretty but worn down. The face of someone carrying too much weight.

Morgan took the photo and studied it. Memorizing every detail. The arch of Beth's eyebrows. The slight crookedness of her nose. The line of her jaw. The way her ears sat against her head. Everything. Every single detail mattered. You missed one thing and the whole illusion fell apart. it's like painting a portrait only now you are going to assume that portrait in real life.

"When do we start?" Morgan asked.

"Tomorrow. Beth leaves tomorrow morning. You move in tomorrow afternoon."

Morgan nodded. One day to prepare. One day to get her head right. One day before she became someone else. Someone who was being hunted.

In forty-eight hours, she'd be wearing Beth Warner's face. And hoping the FBI's protection was as good as they promised. And she would have to be that person for three days.

Chapter 4: The face that lies

Beth Warner's apartment was on the west side of Cedar Falls, in a building that had seen better days. Three stories, brick facade, narrow hallways that smelled like old carpet and cooking oil. The kind of place where people minded their own business and didn't ask questions. Perfect for someone trying to stay invisible.

Karen gave Morgan the key and walked her through the setup. They stood in the parking lot while Karen pointed to different positions. "Beth left yesterday afternoon. As far as anyone watching knows, she's still here. We need to keep that illusion going for three more days. Until the trial starts Monday and she can testify from a secure location."

"Who's watching?" Morgan asked, scanning the parking lot. A few cars. A couple of empty spaces. Nothing obvious. But that was the point. Professional surveillance wasn't obvious.

"We don't know for sure. But we have to assume someone is. These people are professionals. They're patient. They know how to watch without being seen." Karen pointed to a white van across the street. "Two of our agents will be in that van. Twenty-four-hour surveillance.

The building next door has a view of the entrance. We've got another agent positioned there with binoculars and a radio."

"Three people. That's it?"

"That's all we can spare without drawing attention. More agents means more of a footprint. More risk of the leak finding out where Beth is." Well, even if it was a thin surveillance team, at least they were there.

Karen handed Morgan a small device that looked like a car key fob. "If anything happens, you press this button. Help will be there in thirty seconds. Maybe less. Don't hesitate. First sign of trouble, you press it."

"Great," Morgan said. "Thirty seconds. That's really comforting." She slipped the device into her pocket, feeling the weight of it. Such a small thing. Her lifeline for the next three days.

"You'll be fine. Just act normal. Go about Beth's routine. We have a schedule for you." Karen handed her a piece of paper with times and activities written in neat handwriting. "Morning coffee at seven. She usually goes to the diner two blocks over. Lunch at noon. She makes it at home, usually a sandwich. Watches TV in the evening. Local news at six. Game shows after that. Keep the lights on. Move around the apartment. Make it look lived in."

Morgan nodded, studying the schedule. It was simple. Mundane. The routine of a single mother trying to keep her head down. Trying to stay safe. "What about her job?"

"She called in sick. Told them she has the flu. You don't need to go anywhere except the diner and maybe the grocery store if you need supplies. Keep it simple. Keep it boring." But if she had the flu, why would she keep going out to the diner for coffee? The thought kept going through Morgan's head.

"Ready?" Karen asked.

Morgan wasn't sure she'd ever be ready for something like this. But she said yes anyway. She'd committed. She'd taken the job. Beth Warner's life depended on this working.

She went inside and climbed the stairs to the second floor. Apartment 2C. The door was plain brown wood, scratched and worn. Morgan unlocked it and stepped inside. The apartment was small. One bedroom, kitchen, living room, bathroom. Clean but cluttered. Toys scattered on the floor. Photos on the walls. A life interrupted.

Morgan walked through each room, getting a feel for the space. The bedroom had a queen bed with a faded quilt. A nightstand with a lamp and a book. The kitchen had dishes in the sink and a shopping list on the refrigerator. The living room had a couch, a TV, and a coffee table covered in magazines. Everything was ordinary. Normal. The home of someone just trying to get by.

She went into the bathroom. Beth Warner's photo was taped to the mirror, just like Karen had promised. Morgan studied it one more time. Blonde hair. Blue eyes. A mole on her right cheek, small but visible. Thin lips. High cheekbones. The face of someone who'd seen too much and couldn't unsee it.

Morgan pressed her palm against the mirror. The glass went cold immediately. She thought about Beth's face. Really thought about it. The exact shape. The exact feeling. The weight of the worry Beth carried in her expression. The fear in her eyes.

The cold rushed through her body, stronger than usual. This wasn't a six-hour job. This was three days. Three days of holding someone else's face. Three days of being someone else completely. Morgan had never held a face this long before. She wasn't sure she could. One thing she knew was that she needed to keep that face for three days or someone's life could be in jeopardy.

But she'd committed. She'd said yes. So she let the cold spread through her chest, her arms, her legs. Let it reach her face and do its work. Her bones ached as they shifted. Her skin pulled and reshaped. The transformation took longer than usual. Almost thirty seconds instead of fifteen. Her body resisting the extended hold it would need to maintain.

When Morgan opened her eyes, Beth Warner looked back at her from the mirror.

Perfect. Every detail. The blonde bob. The blue eyes. The mole. The tired expression. Morgan was Beth Warner now. Completely. Totally.

Karen was waiting in the living room. When she saw Morgan, she nodded slowly. "Perfect. Even I wouldn't know the difference. And I've spent hours with Beth."

"That's the point," Morgan said in Beth's voice. Different from her own. Lower. Raspier. The voice of someone who'd cried too much lately.

Karen handed her Beth's phone and wallet. "Everything you need is here. Her ID, credit cards, phone contacts. Call if you need anything. Otherwise, we'll check in twice a day. Once in the morning, once at night."

"And if someone comes after me?" Morgan asked. She needed to hear it again. Needed to believe it.

"Press the button. We'll handle it. You have my word." Karen put a hand on Morgan's shoulder. Beth's shoulder. "Thank you for doing this. You're saving a good woman's life."

Then she left. Morgan locked the door behind her and stood in the middle of Beth Warner's apartment. The silence felt heavy. Oppressive. This was her life now. For the next seventy-two hours, she was Beth Warner. A woman in hiding. A woman in danger. A woman whose children needed her to survive this.

Morgan walked to the window and looked down at the street. The white van was still there. She couldn't see inside through the tinted windows, but she knew they were watching. Two agents. Waiting. Ready.

She hoped they were as good as Karen promised. She hoped thirty seconds would be fast enough. Because for the next three days, that van was the only thing standing between Morgan and whoever was hunting Beth Warner.

Chapter 5: Echos in the mirror

The first night was quiet. Too quiet. Morgan sat on Beth's couch and waited for something to happen. Nothing did. The hours crawled by. She checked the windows every thirty minutes. The street below stayed empty except for the occasional car passing through. The van across the street never moved. No lights. No visible activity. Just sitting there in the darkness.

Morgan didn't sleep. Couldn't. Holding Beth's face took constant concentration. Not active concentration, exactly. More like background effort. Like keeping a muscle tensed. If she relaxed too much, the face would start to slip. She could feel it even now, the slight pull at the edges. The cold wanting to let go. Her real face wanting to emerge.

So she stayed awake, watching TV with the volume low. Some late-night talk show she didn't really watch. Then infomercials. Then local news when morning finally came. Keeping Beth's features locked in place took energy. Mental energy. Physical energy. By morning, her head ached. Her whole body ached.

The face was holding, but it felt heavier now. Like wearing a mask made of ice that was slowly melting. Like something that wanted to slide off but she was forcing it to stay put. Morgan touched Beth's face with Beth's hands. The features felt solid enough. But she could sense the strain underneath. The effort it took.

She made coffee and checked Beth's schedule. Seven a.m. Morning coffee at the diner. Morgan looked out the window. The sun was just coming up. The street was starting to wake. A few early commuters. A jogger. Normal morning in Cedar Falls.

Morgan didn't go to the diner. Too risky on the first day. Instead, she made do with the instant coffee in Beth's kitchen. Spent the day moving around the apartment. Making breakfast. Doing dishes. Sitting by the window with a book. Watching TV. All the normal things Beth would do, especially if she had called in and said she had the flu. Anyone watching would see a woman going about her day. Sick with the flu but recovering. Nothing unusual.

Karen called at noon, right on schedule. "Everything okay?"

"Quiet," Morgan said. "Too quiet."

"That's good. Means they haven't found you yet. Keep it that way. Two more days."

But it didn't feel good. It felt like waiting for a storm. You knew it was coming. You could feel it in the air. The pressure building. You just didn't know when it would hit.

The storm came on the second night, just after nine o'clock. Morgan was watching TV when she heard footsteps in the hallway outside. Slow, deliberate footsteps. Someone trying to be quiet but not quite quiet enough. The old building had thin walls, creaky floors. You couldn't hide sound completely.

Morgan muted the TV and listened. The footsteps stopped outside her door. She grabbed the panic button Karen had given her. Her thumb hovered over it. Waiting. Her heart was pounding so hard she could hear it in her ears.

She heard metal scraping against metal. Someone was picking the lock. Professional. Quiet. Using tools. This wasn't some random break-in. This was planned. This was what they'd been waiting for.

Morgan pressed the button. Once. Hard. The device vibrated slightly in her hand. Signal sent. Help was coming. Thirty seconds. Maybe less. She just had to survive thirty seconds.

The door opened slowly. A man stepped inside. Tall, well over six feet. Broad shoulders filling the doorway. Wearing all black. Black pants. Black jacket. Black gloves. Even a black mask covering the lower half of his face. Professional. This was someone who knew what they were doing. Someone who'd done this before.

He saw Morgan and stopped. His eyes locked onto hers. Then he smiled. She could see it in his eyes even though his mouth was covered. Cold eyes. Dead eyes. The eyes of someone who killed for money and felt nothing about it.

"Beth Warner," he said. His voice was calm. Almost friendly. Like they were meeting at a party instead of him breaking into her apartment to kill her. "We've been looking for you. You've been very hard to find."

Morgan didn't move. Didn't speak. Thirty seconds. Karen said thirty seconds. How long had it been? Ten seconds? Fifteen? Time felt strange. Too fast and too slow at the same time.

The man walked toward her. Casual. Unhurried. Like he had all the time in the world. "You shouldn't have talked to the FBI. That was a mistake. Mr. Patterson doesn't like people who talk. Causes problems. Bad for business."

Morgan backed toward the window. Her mind was racing. Where were the agents? Where was the help? The window was behind her. Second floor. Too high to jump. She was trapped.

Twenty seconds. Had to be twenty seconds by now. Maybe twenty-five. Almost there. Almost.

The man pulled something from his jacket. A gun. Black, small, professional. The kind with a silencer attached. Silent. Clean. No neighbors would hear anything. No one would know until it was too late. No, he didn't bother having a towel and wrapping the gun in it or putting it inside some kind of plastic bottle. He brought the right equipment with him.

"Nothing personal," he said, raising the gun. "Just business." What was the expression, "cool as a cucumber"?

The door exploded inward. Actually exploded. The wood splintering as it crashed open. Three FBI agents rushed in, guns drawn, shouting. The man turned, surprised for the first time. His gun swung toward the agents. One of them tackled him before he could fire. The gun clattered across the floor, sliding under the couch.

Morgan pressed herself against the wall, heart pounding, trying to make herself small. The agents had the man on the ground now. Hands behind his back. One agent was reading him his rights. The words sounded distant, muffled, like Morgan was hearing them underwater.

Karen appeared in the doorway. She looked at Morgan, then at the man on the floor. Her face was calm. Professional. Like this was all according to plan. Which, Morgan realized, it probably was.

"You okay?" Karen asked, walking over to Morgan.

Morgan nodded. She wasn't sure if that was true, but she said it anyway. Her hands were shaking. Her whole body was shaking. She couldn't make it stop.

The agents dragged the man out of the apartment. He didn't struggle. Didn't say anything. Just went quietly, like he knew the game was over. Like he'd known the risks when he took the job.

Karen stayed behind. "We got him," she said. "That's the guy we've been after. Professional hitman. Works for Patterson's organization. He's going away for a long time. Breaking and entering, attempted murder, weapons charges. We've got him on everything."

"Great," Morgan said. Her voice didn't sound like Beth's anymore. It was shaking too much. Her hands were still shaking. She couldn't stop them. Couldn't control anything.

"You did good," Karen said. "Really good. Beth Warner is safe because of you. Her kids still have a mother because you were brave enough to do this."

Morgan looked at her. Really looked at her. Karen's face was calm. Satisfied. Almost pleased. And in that moment, Morgan understood. "Was this the plan all along? Use me as bait?"

Karen didn't answer right away. She looked down at her shoes. Then back up at Morgan. "We needed to draw him out. This was the only way. We couldn't catch him without proof. Without him actually making a move."

"You lied to me. You used me."

"We protected you. You were never in real danger. We were thirty seconds away. Just like I promised. And it worked. That's what matters."

Morgan felt Beth's face slipping. The adrenaline, the fear, the anger. All of it had broken her concentration completely. The cold was spreading through her body again, but this time it was pulling the face away. Letting it go. Her real features emerging underneath.

Karen watched Morgan's features shift back to normal. The blonde hair darkening to auburn. The blue eyes changing to hazel. The shape of her face transforming. In thirty seconds, Beth Warner was gone completely. Morgan Hayes stood in her place.

"We'll have your payment by tomorrow," Karen said. "Fifty thousand. As promised. You earned it."

"I don't want it," Morgan said. Her own voice now. Higher than Beth's. Different tone. Different everything.

"What?"

"Keep the money. I don't want anything from you." Morgan walked past Karen, heading for the door. She needed to leave. Needed to get out of this apartment. Away from the FBI. Away from Karen and her calm face and her lies.

"Ms. Hayes—"

Morgan didn't stop. Didn't look back. She just left.

Chapter 6: The man who finds people

Morgan spent two days inside her apartment after returning home while she stayed locked out of the world. She refused to pick up any phone calls and she ignored all her incoming messages. She spent her time watching the street outside from her window seat. The assignment had been more unsettling than Morgan ever dreamed it could have been. She could have been killed, and they didn't bother telling her that was a possibility. They'd used her as bait. How do you do that to someone? She thought about it and decided it was how the organization functioned. It wasn't something she wanted to ever repeat again.

The man with the gun kept appearing in her mind while she remembered his deadly stare which treated her as a mere assignment to eliminate. Yes, she was just an assignment.

She had faced threats before when her past involved dangerous situations with former boyfriends and dangerous individuals. The situation felt different from all her previous experiences. The person who killed for payment had a professional approach to his work. He went about it as though he was doing something as innocuous as grocery shopping.

Karen had always been aware of the situation from the start. The fifty thousand dollars she offered served as her reason to seek Morgan's assistance. They probably figured that if they offered her enough money, she would agree to participate.

Morgan reached out to touch the bathroom mirror. Her reflection showed a worn-out face with pale skin. She attempted to recall the sensation of being her authentic self while avoiding the disguise of another person.

Jenna stood outside Morgan's door on the third day after Morgan had been hiding inside.

"Morgan, do you need help right now?"

Morgan stepped out of her room to face Jenna, who held two coffee cups in her hands. Generous and empathic as ever, she was there for her friend.

"Your appearance looks completely awful to me," Jenna said.

"Thanks."

"Want to talk about it?"

Morgan took a coffee from Jenna before sitting down on the couch. Jenna sat beside her on the couch. She kept quiet instead of asking any questions. She sat waiting for Morgan to begin talking.

"I accepted a federal job, which turned out to be a disaster."

"How bad?"

"Guy with a gun bad." She almost gave a sardonic laugh at that point, but she stopped herself.

Jenna's eyes widened. "Jesus, Morgan."

"I'm okay because the FBI managed to capture him. The FBI used me as their bait for the operation. Can you imagine that?"

Jenna stayed silent before she put her hand on Morgan's shoulder. "You understand that you have the option to stop working and find a regular job and experience regular life."

"I can't."

"Why not?"

Morgan focused on her coffee while she spoke. "People need my assistance because they can't escape their situations like Claire and others do."

"People like Beth Warner?"

Morgan remained silent about the matter. The FBI had used her as their bait during the operation, which resulted in Beth Warner surviving because of her actions. Morgan wasn't going to forget that.

"So what now?" Jenna asked.

"I'll continue working on small assignments while avoiding all federal cases." The jobs she took did have a degree of danger but nothing like this.

Jenna gave a nod of agreement to the plan. "Sounds like a plan."

Morgan checked her phone which lit up with an incoming message from an unknown sender.

"I need help and my friend give me your contact information." Whoever had given this person her phone number, she knew they understood what type of work she accepted, and she was curious to hear what this person needed.

Morgan studied the message while her mind processed the situation. A new person needed her assistance to vanish from existence.

"What is it?" Jenna asked.

"Work," Morgan said. She drank her coffee before sending a response to the message.

"I'll contact you with a phone call during the next hour."

Chapter 7: The decoy

Morgan took a week off after the Beth Warner job. No calls. No faces. Just herself. She needed some time to pull herself together, think things over, and consider her next assignment.

She spent the days in her apartment above the bakery, listening to the sounds of the bakers below. The smell of fresh bread rose through the floorboards every morning. It was comforting. Real. Something that didn't change. She even enjoyed the loud banter that went on with them as they went about kneading their bread, pulling it in and out of the ovens, and putting it on trays.

Jenna worked at the bakery. She'd been Morgan's roommate for two years, and she knew about Morgan's ability. She was one of the few people who did. Morgan trusted her not to ask too many questions. After all, it was a bit complicated about how all of this came to be and she didn't have the energy to sit down and have one of those conversations now.

On the seventh day, Morgan's phone rang. Unknown number. She almost didn't answer. But something made her pick up. Curiosity, after all, did have its motivation.

"Morgan Hayes?" A woman's voice. Older. Scared.

"Yeah."

"My name is Helen Cross. I got your number from a friend. She said you help people."

"What do you need?" It was a normal question that Morgan always asked at the beginning of one of these conversations.

"It's not for me. It's for my daughter. She's in trouble."

Morgan sat down. "What kind of trouble?"

"She testified against her boss. He was embezzling money from the company. Now he's threatening her. He has connections. Dangerous people."

Morgan closed her eyes. Another witness. Another person who spoke up and paid the price. But another interaction with "dangerous" people.

"I'm listening," Morgan said.

"She needs to disappear for a while. Until the trial. Maybe a few weeks. Can you help her?"

A few weeks. Morgan had never held a face that long. The longest she'd ever done was three days with Beth Warner, and that had nearly broken her. How could she ever do something for a few weeks? It might not work. How could she promise it would work if she had never done it before?

"I can't hold someone's face for weeks," Morgan said. "That's not how it works." She had to be honest with this woman.

"What if you just helped her get away? Wore her face long enough for her to leave town?" Okay, now it was sounding like less than a few weeks.

That was different. That was doable. Morgan thought about it for a moment.

"How soon?" Morgan asked.

"Tomorrow. If you can."

Morgan looked at the mirror across the room. Her own face looked back. Auburn hair, hazel eyes. The scar on her chin.

She'd promised herself no more dangerous jobs. No more federal cases. Just simple work. Helping people escape bad relationships.

But Helen Cross's daughter wasn't a federal case. She was just someone who needed help. Someone who'd done the right thing and was being punished for it.

"What's your daughter's name?" Morgan asked.

"Nicole. Nicole Cross."

"Tell Nicole to meet me tomorrow at ten. I'll text you the address."

"Thank you," Helen said. Her voice broke. "Thank you so much." How can you not help a mother whose daughter is in trouble?

Morgan hung up and stared at her phone. She was doing it again. Taking on someone else's danger. Wearing someone else's life.

But maybe that was okay. Maybe that was what she was meant to do.

Chapter 8:
Between faces

Nicole Cross showed up the next day at ten sharp. She was young, maybe twenty-five, with red hair and freckles. She looked like someone who'd never expected to be in this kind of trouble. In fact, she looked like all of those facial cleanser commercials with those scrubbed-clean American girls.

"My mom told me about you," Nicole said. "She said you can look like anyone."

"That's right."

"How does it work?" Morgan wondered if that really mattered, if she needed to have somebody to substitute for her in order to help her get out of danger. But she understood.

"I borrow your face for a few hours. Long enough for you to get out of town. While I'm you, anyone watching will think you're still here."

Nicole sat down on the couch. "This sounds crazy."

"It is," Morgan said. "But it works."

"How long can you hold my face?"

"Usually six to eight hours. Sometimes longer if I push it. Why?" Was someone else not being honest with her about how long this job would take or what it would truly entail?

Nicole looked down at her hands. "My mom said you might be able to hold it for a week. I need to stay hidden until the trial. That's seven days from now."

Morgan's stomach tightened. "I've never held a face that long. The longest I've done is three days, and that nearly killed me."

"But could you try?" The pleading note in her voice was pushing Morgan to agree, even though she knew this was going to be an extended trial of just how long she could hold a face.

Morgan looked at Nicole. She was scared. Not just scared. Terrified. Someone was hunting her, and she had nowhere else to go.

"What happens if I say no?" Morgan asked.

Nicole's eyes filled with tears. "Then I run. And hope they don't find me."

Morgan thought about Beth Warner. About Claire Martinez. About all the people she'd helped over the years. People who needed to disappear. People who needed someone else to take their place, just for a little while.

Seven days. That was insane. That was impossible. Maybe it was possible; maybe it was impossible. Morgan didn't know.

But Morgan had never walked away from someone who needed help. No, she'd never refused to help someone yet.

"Okay," Morgan said. "I'll try. But I can't promise I'll make it the full seven days." Better to have it all out in the open. No promises made.

Nicole let out a shaky breath. "Thank you. I don't know how to repay you."

"Just stay safe. That's enough."

They spent the next hour going over the plan. Nicole would hide at her aunt's house two states away. Morgan would stay in Nicole's apartment, acting like everything was normal. Going to work, running errands, living Nicole's life.

"My boss's people are watching," Nicole said. "They'll know if I leave town. That's why we need this to work."

Morgan nodded. "Show me your apartment. I need to know the layout."

Nicole's apartment was small. One bedroom, kitchen, bathroom. Simple. Normal. The kind of place a twenty-five-year-old accountant would live.

Morgan went into the bathroom and looked at the mirror. Nicole stood behind her.

"Ready?" Morgan asked.

"Yeah."

Morgan pressed her palm against the mirror. The glass went cold. She thought about Nicole's face. Red hair, freckles, green eyes. Young. Scared.

The cold rushed through her body, and Morgan felt her features shift. When she opened her eyes, Nicole Cross stared back at her from the mirror.

Behind her, the real Nicole gasped.

"It's weird, seeing yourself like this," Nicole said.

"You get used to it," Morgan said in Nicole's voice.

They traded clothes. Nicole gave Morgan her keys, her phone, her wallet. Everything Morgan would need to be Nicole Cross for the next seven days. They even went over the work Morgan would be expected to do and which would require no special knowledge, so that Morgan could do it if needed. No sense in having her mess up on the job and quickly be discovered.

"Stay safe," Morgan said.

"You too."

Nicole left through the back exit. Morgan locked the door and stood in the middle of the apartment. For the next seven days, this was her life. She was Nicole Cross now.

And somewhere out there, dangerous people were watching. Dangerous people again, and she had told herself she wouldn't get into this kind of situation.

Chapter 9: The face you choose

The first three days were hard. The fourth day was harder. By the fifth day, Morgan wasn't sure she could keep going. She was questioning whether or not she should have taken this assignment even though the young woman was in such desperate straits.

Holding Nicole's face for that long felt like wearing a suit of frozen metal. Her bones ached constantly. Her head throbbed with a pain that went deeper than her skull, like something cold had wrapped itself around her brain and squeezed. Every morning, she looked in the mirror and had to force Nicole's features back into place. They kept slipping, fading at the edges like watercolor in rain. The effort was exhausting.

The mirror felt different now too. When she pressed her hand to the glass each morning, the cold came slower, weaker. Like trying to start a car in winter when the battery was dying. She had to concentrate harder, focus longer, just to maintain what should have been automatic. Morgan didn't know quite what was happening but it appeared that she was beyond her range here.

But she kept going. She went to Nicole's job at the accounting firm on the third floor of a building downtown. Fluorescent lights. Gray cubicles. The smell of burnt coffee and printer toner. She made small talk with coworkers whose names she'd memorized from Nicole's notes. She bought groceries at the store Nicole always went to, cooked dinner the way Nicole would cook it, watched the same TV shows Nicole watched. Everything Nicole would do.

The routine helped. Gave her something to focus on besides the constant ache in her body and the way Nicole's face kept trying to slip away.

And every night, she checked the windows. Watching for the people who were watching her. They were always there. Different cars. Different faces. But always there. Patterson's people. Making sure Nicole stayed put. Making sure she didn't run. They were waiting for the trial day.

On the sixth day, one of them made contact.

Morgan was leaving the grocery store, plastic bags cutting into her fingers, when a man approached her. Mid-forties, expensive, custom-made suit, cold eyes that looked right through her. He moved like someone who was used to getting what he wanted.

"Nicole Cross?" he said. His voice was smooth. Professional. The kind of voice that made threats sound like suggestions.

Morgan's heart pounded so hard she thought other people could hear it. But she kept her expression calm. Bored, even. The way someone would look at a stranger interrupting their grocery trip. "Yes?"

"My name is David Brennan. I work for Mr. Patterson. I think you know who that is."

Patterson. Nicole's former boss. The man she'd testified against in front of the grand jury. The man who'd stolen millions from pension funds, from people who'd worked their whole lives and had nothing left. The man who wanted Nicole to disappear.

"What do you want?" Morgan asked in Nicole's voice. She'd practiced that voice so many times over the past six days that it came automatically now. The slight upturn at the end of sentences. The way Nicole's accent softened certain words.

"Mr. Patterson would like you to reconsider your testimony. The trial is tomorrow. It's not too late to change your mind." Brennan smiled like he was offering her a reasonable business opportunity. Like he was suggesting she switch phone plans or try a new restaurant.

Morgan felt Nicole's face trying to slip. The stress, the fear, it was making it harder to hold. She forced it back into place and met Brennan's eyes. "I'm not changing anything."

Brennan's smile didn't change, but something shifted in his eyes. Something cold and final. "That's unfortunate. Mr. Patterson was hoping you'd be reasonable. He's a reasonable man himself. He understands that people make mistakes. He understands that sometimes people say things they don't mean, especially when the FBI puts pressure on them." He said it as though he was sympathetic toward her situation and was trying to help.

"I meant every word I said." Morgan affected a no-nonsense tone.

"I see." Brennan glanced at the grocery bags in her hands. "You live alone, don't you, Ms. Cross? That must be difficult. Especially now, with all this stress. It would be terrible if something happened to you. An accident. You know how it is. People get careless when they're under pressure. They forget to lock doors. They don't notice when someone's following them."

Morgan's hands tightened on the grocery bags. "I have nothing more to say to you." She walked past him toward her car, forcing herself not to run. To walk at Nicole's normal pace. Not too fast. Not too slow, but it was excruciatingly difficult.

Brennan grabbed her arm. His grip was tight and painful. "You should be careful, Ms. Cross. Accidents happen. It would be a shame if yours happened before you could reconsider."

Morgan pulled her arm free. The grocery bags swung, and something inside one of them broke. She heard glass shatter. Felt liquid seeping through the plastic. "Don't touch me."

She got in the car and locked the doors with shaking hands. Brennan stood in the parking lot, hands in his pockets, watching her. Even when she drove away, checking the rearview mirror every few seconds, she could feel his eyes following. Could feel the threat in that calm, professional smile.

Morgan's hands were so tight on the steering wheel that her knuckles turned white. One more day. Just one more day, and Nicole would be safe. The trial would start, and Nicole could testify from a secure location. Nicole would tell the truth, and Patterson would go to prison, and all those people would get some kind of justice.

But Morgan wasn't sure she could hold Nicole's face for one more day. It was slipping faster now. Every hour, she had to concentrate harder to keep it in place. The cold wasn't working the way it should. Her ability felt stretched thin, like a rubber band pulled too far.

When she got back to the apartment, she went straight to the bathroom. Left the leaking grocery bags on the kitchen counter. Nicole's face looked back from the mirror, but it was fading. The edges were blurry, indistinct, like someone had smeared the image. Morgan pressed her hands to the glass and forced the features to sharpen.

The cold rushed through her body, but it felt different now. Weaker. Like her ability was running out. Like there was only so much she could ask of it before it gave up entirely.

Morgan again looked at herself in the mirror. Was that Nicole's face? Or was it something in between? She couldn't tell anymore. Couldn't see where Nicole ended and she began.

One more day, she told herself. Just one more day. She'd have to hang on.

Chapter 10: The mirror shows the truth

The seventh day felt like it lasted forever. Morgan barely slept. She spent the night sitting on the couch, forcing Nicole's face to stay in place. Every hour, it slipped a little more. Every hour, it got harder to pull it back. Try as she might, the usual methods were not working as before.

The television played in the background, some late-night show she wasn't watching. The light from the screen flickered across Nicole's apartment, casting shadows that moved and shifted. Outside, a car engine idled for twenty minutes before driving away. Patterson's people. Still watching. Still waiting for her to slip up.

Around three in the morning, Morgan went to the bathroom and looked in the mirror. Nicole's face stared back, but it was wrong. The features were there, but they looked painted on. Artificial. Like a mask that didn't quite fit anymore.

She pressed her hand to the mirror. The cold barely came. Just a whisper of what it should be. A ghost of her ability. She concentrated harder, focusing everything she had on holding the face in place.

It worked. Barely. Nicole's features sharpened again, solidified. But Morgan knew she couldn't keep this up much longer. A few more hours. That was all she had left.

By morning, Morgan wasn't sure what she looked like anymore. She was too scared to check the mirror. Too scared to see what happened when her ability finally gave out.

At eight a.m., her phone rang. Nicole's phone. Morgan stared at it for three rings before answering, her hand shaking so badly she almost dropped it.

"It's me," Nicole said. Her voice was steady. Strong. Nothing like the scared woman who'd come to Morgan's apartment a week ago. "The trial starts in an hour. I'm at the courthouse. Are you okay?"

"Yeah," Morgan lied. Her voice came out rough, tired. "I'm fine."

"I don't believe you," Nicole said. "But thank you. I don't know how you did it. Holding my face for seven days. That's incredible. The FBI agents here, they can't believe it either. They said you saved my life."

Morgan closed her eyes. The apartment swam around her. "Just testify. Tell the truth. That's all that matters."

"I will. And Morgan? Thank you. Really. I'll never forget this." There was a pause, and Morgan heard voices in the background. Official voices. "I have to go. They're calling me in. But thank you. I mean it.

Morgan hung up. She sat on the couch and waited for Nicole's face to slip away. It took twenty minutes. Twenty long minutes of cold spreading through her body, pulling the borrowed features back into storage. She could feel each piece of Nicole's face peeling away. The shape of her nose. The curve of her chin. The color of her eyes. All of it dissolving back into the mirror, back into wherever Morgan kept the faces she borrowed.

When it was over, Morgan looked at herself in the mirror. Auburn hair, longer than she remembered. Hazel eyes that looked exhausted. The scar on her chin from when she'd fallen off her bike when she was so young. She traced it with her finger, feeling the raised skin. Proof that this was her face. Her real face.

She was herself again. But something felt different. Off. Like she'd left a piece of herself behind in Nicole's face. Like holding someone else's identity for that long had worn away some of her own.

Morgan went home in a taxi, too tired to drive. She collapsed on her bed still wearing Nicole's clothes. She slept for fourteen hours straight. No dreams. No nightmares. Just darkness.

When she woke up, Jenna was sitting on the edge of the bed, holding a cup of coffee. The smell of it pulled Morgan back to consciousness.

"You scared me," Jenna said. Her voice was quiet. "I thought you were dead. You didn't answer your phone. You didn't respond to texts. I found you like this. I've been sitting here for an hour making sure you were still breathing."

"I'm okay," Morgan said. Her voice came out hoarse.

"No, you're not. You held that face for too long. I could see it when you came home yesterday. You didn't look like yourself. Your face kept shifting. Like you couldn't quite remember what Morgan Hayes was supposed to look like."

Morgan sat up slowly and took the coffee. The warmth of the mug felt good in her hands. Real. Solid. "It was seven days. That's the longest I've ever done."

"And you can't do it again," Jenna said firmly. "Morgan, listen to me. You're losing yourself in these faces. One day, you're going to shift and not be able to come back. You're going to forget who you are. And then what?"

Morgan looked down at her hands. They were shaking. Had been shaking since she'd let go of Nicole's face. "I know."

"So what are you going to do?"

"I don't know."

Jenna put her hand on Morgan's shoulder. "You don't have to save everyone, you know. You're allowed to say no. You're allowed to have limits."

"But what if they don't have anyone else?" She might be their last hope.

"Then they'll figure it out. People always do. And maybe some of them won't be okay, and that's terrible, but it's not your fault. It's not your responsibility to destroy yourself trying to save everyone who calls you."

Morgan wasn't sure she believed that. But she nodded anyway because Jenna was worried, and Jenna was her best friend, and she didn't want to argue. Not right now. Not when she was this tired.

She spent the next few days resting. No calls. No faces. Just herself. She needed to remember what that felt like. Who she was when she wasn't wearing someone else's life. She watched movies. She read books. She ate food that she liked, not food that Claire or Beth or Nicole would have eaten. She wore her own clothes. She looked in the mirror and saw only her own face looking back.

One night, she stood in front of the bathroom mirror and pressed her palm against the glass. The cold came immediately, eager. Ready to change her. To make her into someone else. To give her any face she wanted.

But Morgan pulled her hand away. Not tonight. Tonight, she was just herself. Morgan Hayes. Auburn hair, hazel eyes, a small scar on her chin. A girl who lived above a bakery and had a roommate named Jenna and an ability she didn't understand.

That was enough. For tonight, that was enough.

A week later, her phone rang. Unknown number. Morgan stared at it for a long moment before answering. Part of her wanted to ignore it. Wanted to let it go to voicemail. Wanted to walk away from all of this. But she couldn't. That wasn't who she was. No matter what Jenna said, no matter how much it hurt, she couldn't turn away from someone who needed help.

"Morgan Hayes?" A young woman's voice. Scared. Desperate. The same tone they all had when they called her. The same shake in the words, the same hope underneath the fear.

"Yeah," Morgan said.

"I got your number from a friend. She said you help people. I need to disappear for a few days. My ex-boyfriend, he's been following me. The police won't do anything. The restraining order doesn't stop him. He shows up everywhere. My work. My apartment. The grocery store. I'm scared. Can you help me?"

Morgan closed her eyes. Another person in trouble. Another person who needed to vanish. Another woman who'd tried all the official channels and found them wanting. Another person the system had failed. The police couldn't help. The courts couldn't help. So she'd found Morgan's number somehow, passed along through some desperate network of women who'd run out of options.

She thought about Jenna's warning. About losing herself in other people's faces. About the danger of holding someone else's identity for too long. About the Beth Warner job and how Karen had used her. About the man with the gun and those thirty seconds that felt like forever. About Nicole's face slipping away and the way she couldn't quite remember what Morgan Hayes was supposed to look like.

But the woman on the phone was scared. Really scared. Morgan could hear it in her voice. The trembling. The desperation. The hope that maybe, just maybe, someone could help her when no one else would.

And Morgan knew what it felt like to be trapped. To need a way out. To have nowhere else to turn. She'd been there. Not in the same way. But she understood. She understood what it meant to be desperate. What it meant to need someone to see you, to believe you, to help you when everyone else had turned away.

"Tell me what you need," Morgan said.

The woman let out a sob of relief. "Thank you. Thank you so much. I don't know what I would have done if you'd said no. I didn't know where else to go."

"Start from the beginning," Morgan said. "Tell me everything."

And as the woman talked, Morgan listened. Taking mental notes. Building a plan. Figuring out how to help. Because no matter what Jenna said, no matter what the FBI had done to her, no matter how dangerous it got, no matter how much it cost her, Morgan couldn't walk away.

This was who she was. The person who helped others disappear. The person who borrowed faces and took on other people's danger. The person who stood between the vulnerable and those who would hurt them. The person who said yes when everyone else said no.

About the Author

P . A. Farrell is an accomplished flash fiction author whose compelling micro-narratives have captivated readers across the literary landscape. With over forty publications in prestigious online journals and literary magazines, Farrell has established herself as a master of the abbreviated form, crafting complete worlds and complex emotions within the constraints of brief word counts.

Her expertise in flash fiction extends beyond individual pieces to comprehensive collections, where she shows remarkable range and consistency in delivering powerful, bite-sized stories that linger long after the last sentence. Each collection showcases her ability to explore diverse themes, characters, and settings while maintaining the precision and impact that define exceptional flash fiction.

Farrell's work resonates with readers who appreciate literature that delivers maximum emotional and intellectual impact in minimal space. Her stories often examine the pivotal moments that define the human experience, capturing the essence of larger truths through carefully chosen details and expertly crafted prose. The breadth of her publication history speaks both to her prolific output and the consistent quality that editors and readers expect from her work.

Through her continued contributions to the flash fiction genre, P.A. Farrell has become a trusted voice for readers seeking literature that respects their time while enriching their understanding of the human condition. Her collections offer the perfect opportunity to experience the full range of her storytelling abilities in a single, cohesive volume.

In her other life, P. A. Farrell is a clinical psychologist who has written several self-help books and continues to contribute to media outlets such as Medium.com and Butterfly, where she posts articles on all aspects of healthcare, mental health, and a variety of other topics. Her Author's Page is here: https://tinyurl.com/4ewdunb8

Books by P. A. Farrell

Snowbound Hearts
  The Secrets We Keep
  The Secrets We Keep 2
  Whispers Across the Sea
  Love by the Latte
  Echoes of Expectation—Waiting
  Unexpected Short Tales of Surprise

A Special Request

I f this book has touched your heart, sparked your curiosity, or simply entertained you along the way, I'd be incredibly grateful if you could take a moment to share your thoughts with a review on Amazon or wherever you discovered this book. Your words not only help other readers find books they'll love, but they also mean the world to authors like me who pour their hearts into every page. Thank you for being part of this journey, and for helping stories find their way to the readers who need them most. Her Author Page on Amazon: https://tinyurl.com/4ewdunb8

www.ingramcontent.com/pod-product-compliance
Lightning Source LLC
Chambersburg PA
CBHW020650130626
46552CB00003B/1489